Have You Got My Purr?

FOR SARAH AND BENJAMIN
—J.W.

FOR GEORGE
—T.W.

ISBN 0-439-24947-3

Text copyright © 1999 by Judy West.
Illustrations copyright © 1999 by Tim Warnes.
All rights reserved.
Published by Scholastic Inc., 555 Broadway, New York, NY 10012,
by arrangement with Dutton Children's Books, a division of Penguin Putnam Inc.
SCHOLASTIC and associated logos are trademarks and/or
registered trademarks of Scholastic Inc.

12 11 10 9 8 7 6 5   2 3 4 5 6/0

Printed in the U.S.A.   08

First Scholastic printing, January 2001

Typography by Alan Carr

Have You Got My Purr?

BY **Judy West**

ILLUSTRATED BY
Tim Warnes

SCHOLASTIC INC.
New York Toronto London Auckland Sydney
Mexico City New Delhi Hong Kong

Kitten was sad. She could mew, she could hiss, and she could yowl, but she couldn't make the noise she liked the best—she couldn't purr.

"Mother," she said, "I think I've lost my purr."

"Little one," her mother replied, "you will find your purr. Just wait and see."

Wait? The determined kitten set out in search of her purr. She decided that Dog might have it.
"Dog," Kitten asked, "have you got my purr?" She climbed onto his belly to listen closely to his answer.

"Woof woof," said the startled dog. "I have a woof, not a purr. Why don't you ask Cow? She may have it."

So Kitten went off to do just that. She found a perch next to the paddock and very near Cow's head. "Cow," Kitten said, looking her right in the eye, "have you got my purr? Dog says you might."

"Moo moo," said Cow quickly.
"I have my moo, but no purr.
Why not ask Pig?"

Kitten slid slowly down the tree and scampered over to the pigpen and up the fence.

"Pig! Have you got my purr?" she called over the snuffling of the piglets.

So Kitten followed the sounds of splashing and found the Ducks enjoying their day-long bath.

"Ducks, I've asked Dog and Cow and Pig, but they don't seem to have it. Have *you* got my purr?"

"Quack quack," said the Ducks. "Does that sound like a purr? We quack."

One duck offered kindly, "Why not ask Mouse?"

This would be tricky, but Kitten really wanted her purr back. She scooted over to the mouse hole, got down on her belly, and wiggled through.

"Don't be afraid, Mouse," said Kitten very quietly, "You see, I am searching for something. Have you got my purr?"

"Squeak squeak," said Mouse nervously. "I have my squeak, Kitten, but I do not have your purr. Have you asked squeak— I mean, Sheep?"

A little discouraged and very tired, Kitten hung her head and wandered over to the field. "Sheep," she sighed, "I have lost my purr. Mouse says you might have it. Have you got my purr?"

"Baa baa," said Sheep. "I haven't got your purr, little one. My old baa is all I have. Why not ask Owl?"

So Kitten stumbled sleepily over to
Owl's tree and said, "Owl, I have searched
all day. I'm so tired. Have you got my purr?"
"Hoot hoot," Owl said. "Silly kitten, I have
a hoot, not a purr. Why don't you go back to
your mother? I'm sure you'll find your purr
there."

Kitten couldn't believe it. Has Mother had my purr all along? she wondered.

She rushed back to the barn to call out her question one last time. "Mother, have you got my purr?"

"Oh, sweet thing," said her mother tenderly, "no one can take your purr. It's inside you. You hear it when you're happy. Come here and listen."

So Kitten snuggled next to her mother, and suddenly . . .

. . . there it was!
The dog did not woof.
The cow did not moo.
The pig did not oink.
The ducks did not quack.
The mouse did not squeak.
The sheep did not baa.
The owl did not hoot.

They all watched from the door and listened silently to the most perfect purr they had ever heard.

PURR

PURR